MOUSEY MOUSEY AND THE WITCHES' SPELLS

Second Edition

by Heather Flood

SECOND EDITION
PUBLISHED BY Antony Flood,
Sportsworld Communications, January 2018.
Previously published by MyVoice Publishing, October 2015.
Copyright © Heather Flood
Heather Flood asserts the moral right to be identified as the
author of this work.

Illustrations by Vicky Rosenthal
Cover design by Nicky Shearsby from an
illustration by Vicky Rosenthal.

ISBN-13: 978-1981575565
ISBN-10: 1981575561

DEDICATION

This book is dedicated to my family, Emma, Lee, Kirsty and James, grandchildren Gabrielle-Antonia, Ashlee and Samuel, and my lovely husband Tony.

Gabrielle was my main inspiration for writing these Mousey Mousey adventures with her love of the colour pink and her repeated requests, together with those of Ashlee, for me to read them bedtime stories.

Tony's belief in me and the enormous help and advice he has provided as a fellow author have also been a tremendous source of encouragement.

I was delighted when Tony turned one of my ideas into his own children's fantasy book The Secret Potion, which has been hailed as the ideal follow up to Harry Potter.

My thanks go to actor Jeffrey Holland, authors Jay Dixon and Jill Rutherford, Angela Warren and Kirsty Stephens for their positive reviews.

I am also grateful to Vicky Rosenthal for her wonderful illustrations, and to the advice given by publisher Rex Sumner.

4

REVIEWS

A heroine is born! Mousey Mousey is so good they named her twice! A delightful children's story character that will appeal to children everywhere. Here are dilemmas, bullies, friends, creepy-crawlies, morals - all the things that make up a good children's story. Never mind the children, I loved it!

Jeffrey Holland, actor of Hi-de-Hi! fame.

Mousey Mousey is a delightful character who young children will easily identify with, and her exciting adventures always end with a moral. But above all these stories are fun! The witch Agatha is suitably ugly and scary- though not too scary! - and her ideas of good food will have children wriggling in delight.

Jay Dixon, author, The Romance Fiction of Mills & Boon 1909-1990s.

Children should love these delightful tales about Mousey Mousey - she's such a sweet little mouse, I fell for her straight away. There are morals, scary moments and, above all, bags of fun – these are ideal bedtime stories. Maybe Mousey Mousey will be the next Hello Kitty - fighting bad with good and charming us in the process! And maybe she will become the most loveable children's character since Beatrix Potter's Peter Rabbit.

Jill Rutherford, author, Cherry Blossoms, Sushi and Takarazuka, seven years in Japan.

Mousey Mousey is adorable. My five-year-old grand-daughter Madison loves her as much as Julia Donaldson's The Gruffalo and Jacqueline Wilson's Glubbslyme. I think Heather Flood has come up with the best children's book since Enid Blyton's Noddy and Beatrix Potter's The Tale of Peter Rabbit.

Angela Warren, grandmother from Maidenhead, Berks.

My friends and I are delighted that Heather Flood has written such wonderful stories for our children to enjoy. All children should adore Mousey Mousey, Molly Mole, Rachel Rabbit, Ben Badger and Mousey's other friends. And they will laugh so much about the antics of the naughty witch Agatha and her daughter Bernice - mine did! The writing in these magical stories is simply spellbinding and the drawings and front cover are also delightful.

Kirsty Stephens, mother.

The Naughty Witch

The Naughty Witch

Mousey Mousey lived in a small pink cottage by a river in the tiny village of Dobble.

Everything inside her home was a lovely shade of pink - including the wallpaper, her carpets and armchairs. Her curtains had pink stripes and her cushions were all pink and fluffy.

The little white mouse had just finished dyeing the hair on top of her head pink and stood looking at it in the mirror, with her pink hair-dryer in her hand. 'I think I will go and show my friend Molly Mole my new hair colour,' she thought.

Molly lived in the cottage next to Mousey Mousey, but when she got there no one was in, so the mouse sat by the river which ran in front of their homes and took off her shoes to soak her feet. It was a lovely sunny day in Dobble and she began to doze.

Suddenly Mousey Mousey felt cold and opened her eyes. There in the sky, flying above where she was sitting, was a large witch, staring down at her from a broomstick. Mousey Mousey picked up her shoes and ran back to her cottage.

She looked out of her window and was pleased to see that the witch had gone. She then went into the bathroom, dried her feet and put on her new pink slippers.

Mousey Mousey had invited Molly Mole and her other friends, Rachel Rabbit and Ben Badger, to come round that afternoon for a cup of tea and a slice of her home-made pink iced sponge cake.

They always chatted about things they were going to do in the village and were planning to hold several events including a fête and a party in the summer.

Ben Badger liked growing roses and Mousey Mousey had a lovely pink climbing rose in her back garden which Ben had given her for her birthday. But she spent most of her time making cakes and biscuits.

Molly loved to paint and Rachel, who had six little bunnies, enjoyed knitting so they would all have lots of things to sell at the fête.

The little mouse was just putting the cake on a tray when there was a loud knock at the door. She went to open it, thinking that one of her friends had arrived early.

Her mouth dropped open when she saw a large witch standing there - the same one who had given her a fright earlier.

Fear gripped the little mouse again as the elderly witch stood towering over her.

"Hello, dear," said the old woman, who was just putting her broomstick up against the wall. The witch was so large she had to bend down to speak to Mousey Mousey. She was dressed all in black and wore a big, pointed hat. She had an ugly hairy wart on the end of her nose and very long, sharp finger nails.

"C-c-can I help you?" stuttered the little mouse, startled at seeing the witch again.

The old hag leaned on the door and said in her croaky voice: "Yes, dear, can I come in for a minute as I am very tired?

"I was flying back from a potions meeting in the Black Mountains to my home at Witchy Poo Corner when I saw your very bright pink cottage and you running into it. So I thought I would take a short break."

As she spoke, she took out her wand and waved it. There was a PING – and the witch shrunk so that she was now only slightly bigger than Mousey Mousey. This meant she was small enough to get through the cottage door.

"I have a terrible headache, dear. Perhaps I could have a drink of water to take with the toad egg extra strong tablets I have in my bag. If I can come in for a rest and take two of my pills my headache will soon go away."

"Yes, yes, of course - please come in and maybe you would like some tea instead of water," replied Mousey Mousey in a soft voice, feeling sorry for the old witch, although she was also slightly scared of her.

The witch entered, took out a pair of · dark sunglasses from her pocket, and put them on over her hairy wart.

"It's so bright in here, dear," she muttered. "I will have to wear these glasses or my headache will get worse." She looked at all the pink and wrinkled her nose in disgust.

As the witch walked in BLACK footprints began to appear on Mousey Mousey's pink carpet. The little mouse did not notice because she was leading the way into the lounge. "My name is Agatha," croaked the witch, treating the mouse to a small smile, and showing two rows of black teeth. Agatha pushed the sunglasses further up her nose and chose the largest armchair to sit in.

When she sat down the fluffy cushion behind her back turned purple with black spots. The witch's eyes twinkled mischievously. Mousey Mousey did not see what had happened as she was walking into the kitchen to make the tea.

"Can you put 10 spoonfuls in the pot, dear," called out the witch. "I like my tea strong."

Mousey Mousey was shocked and, instead of 10 spoonfuls, she decided to put in only five. She was sure that the old witch had made a mistake, and she did not want her tea to taste awful.

When it was ready the mouse put the teapot on a tray with a few of her special biscuits, leaving the pink sponge cake for her friends' visit. 'They will be surprised when they come and see a WITCH sitting in my armchair, drinking tea,' she thought.

Feeling pleased with herself, Mousey Mousey went into the lounge and placed the tray on a little side table next to the witch. But, as she poured out the tea, something caught her eye. "OH! WHATEVER HAS HAPPENED TO MY CUSHION?" she cried, noticing the purple colour.

"I'm glad you like it, dear," chuckled Agatha. "I cannot imagine how anyone could bear to live in a cottage with so much pink - I will not stay long because it makes me feel quite ill.

"I'll just take my toad egg headache pills and be off home. It's been a long tiring day."

Mousey Mousey then saw the black footprints all over her pink carpet. She was annoyed, and sat tapping her foot. But she did not say anything in case the witch turned more of her things purple or black....or perhaps changed her into a toad.

She poured out the tea and offered the witch the biscuits. "I hope you like my home-made biscuits," she said. "The recipe has been in my family for generations."

The witch took a bite and wrinkled her nose again to express her dislike for them, which made Mousey Mousey even more cross.

Plucking up her courage, the mouse declared: "I actually LIKE pink in my home, as it looks warm and makes me feel happy. What colours do you like?"

The witch scratched her big hairy wart, and laughed. "Well, black, of course, dear, with a touch of purple here and there. Why don't you let me show you how lovely and dark I can make it in here?" As she said this, the tea-cup she was holding turned black. "A few spiders and cobwebs would be splendid, don't you think? Spiders are such sweet little creatures. I think I have a few under my hat, and they tickle."

Mousey Mousey somehow managed not to scream. Instead, she said politely: "OH NO! That's very generous of you, but you are tired - and I like it the way it is, thank you." She forced a smile and tried to look relaxed in front of the witch, but all the time she wished the old woman would leave –

and hopefully not make any more black footprints on the carpet on the way out.

When Agatha had finished her tea, taken her pills and eaten all the biscuits she got up suddenly. "Well, I must go now, dear - thank you for the tea, although it was weaker than I usually have. Ten spoonfuls of tea, left in the pot for about six minutes, is how I like it - then there are lots of tea leaves for me to read."

Agatha went to the door, spreading more BLACK footprints over the carpet. Mousey Mousey put her little hands over her mouth to stop herself shouting at the witch.

"Oh, and the biscuits were a bit too sugary for me," the witch continued. "I don't suppose I will be coming this way again or I would give you my recipe for bat wing biscuits, and my spider leg cheese straws are yummy – there are so crunchy.

"My daughter Bernice loves them. I suppose I could make a special batch for you and fly them over."

The witch turned round to look at Mousey Mousey with a cunning grin. She obviously enjoyed causing mischief. "Please d-d-don't go to any t-t-trouble - there is no need to come back, it's probably a l-l-long way," stammered Mousey Mousey, trying to get rid of the old hag without making her cross.

"Well thank you once again, my dear," cackled the witch. "I must go now as my daughter Bernice will worry if I am not home soon.

"You would probably get on well with Bernice as she has funny ways like you. She will not even try my frog's spew custard, and she likes bright colours occasionally - she is a strange girl. But you can't beat black..." Then, remembering how she had changed the cushion, she added: "With a touch of purple, of course."

The witch went outside, changed herself to her normal size and got on her broomstick. Then, with a wave goodbye, she flew up into the sky, higher and higher, but just before disappearing, she looked back, took out her wand and said a few words. Finally, with a large grin she flew on her way. Feeling happy that the witch had gone, Mousey Mousey went inside her little cottage, and pushed the door closed with a CLONK. She walked into the lounge, but when she saw what the witch had done she threw her hands up in horror and SCREAMED.

All the pink had gone - nearly everything in her house was now a ghastly black. It all looked horrible.

Mousey Mousey sat down in the middle of the room, holding one of her purple cushions and sobbed. Her bright, pretty little cottage was now dark and ugly - it looked just like somewhere a witch would live. In the corner of her lounge she found SIX BLACK SPIDERS - and there were cobwebs everywhere.

When her friends Molly, Rachel and Ben arrived they were amazed to see all the black things in Mousey Mousey's cottage, and she let them all put their arms round her until she stopped crying. But soon she started again!

"What shall I do?" howled the little mouse as they sat on her awful black chairs.

Ben the Badger eased his stout frame out of his chair and went into the kitchen to make the tea. When he returned he put a plate of her delicious biscuits on the dark, unwelcoming table (he had presumably decided that it would upset Mousey Mousey more to see her lovely cake with the now horrid black icing, so he left it in the kitchen). But she was not hungry.

They all sat sipping tea and trying to find ways of cheering up Mousey Mousey, yet it was useless because the sad little mouse was so upset.

Mousey Mousey had tried to sweep the spiders away with a feather duster, but they ran across the floor or up the curtains!

"I will stay with you tonight," whispered Molly Mole to her friend as she took the cups and plates into the dark kitchen to wash up. "I think you ought to have a little sleep now as you have suffered quite a shock." Mousey Mousey thanked her friends and went into her now very spooky black bedroom.

She woke up next day, hoping that it had all been a dream, but as she opened her eyes she saw her black curtains, purple pillows and sheets and her little black hair-dryer. She couldn't stop herself crying again.

Molly Mole came in with a bowl full of cornflakes and a glass of milk on a tray, which she almost dropped as she tripped over a pair of black slippers.

But Mousey Mousey could not even raise a smile at her short-sighted friend's stumble - neither could she bring herself to eat anything. When Molly went home the mouse sat in one of her armchairs and held her head, tears plopping down her cheeks onto her apron. Yesterday the apron had pink little butterflies all over it - now they were black and purple.

Mousey Mousey took off the apron, threw it on the floor and ran into her bedroom where she lay sobbing on her bed.

Then she had a great idea. She rushed to the shops and bought new pink cushions and curtains, a pink hair-dryer and two pink rugs, yet the moment she took her new things inside her cottage they all turned black again.

Week after week she bought little pink things, but the witch had put a spell on everything that came into the cottage and Mousey Mousey could not change it.

Her eyes had big bags under them because she could not sleep. And the little mouse spent most days sitting by the river bank watching the sky, fearing that the old witch would return to do more horrible things.

At least the outside of her cottage was still pink and she had all the pink flowers in her garden to look at, but Mousey Mousey worried that if Agatha came back she might change these, too!

What if one day she opened her door and all the beautiful colours in the garden had gone, to be replaced by just BLACK AND PURPLE? No more green trees with pink blossom in the spring, or her favourite pink roses.

Many weeks went by and one day, as Mousey Mousey was hanging up her black washing and about to go back into her dark cottage, she noticed something flying towards her. She trembled as another witch, much younger than the first, landed her broomstick at the bottom of her garden. The young witch had a long, elegant, black velvet coat and wore her very straight hair pulled back away from her eyes. She did not have a hat. She smiled at Mousey Mousey and said: "Hello, my name is Bernice. I believe you had a visit from my mother, Agatha, some time ago and you kindly invited her in for tea and biscuits. Can I come in, too, because I have also flown a long way and need to rest?"

'OH, NO,' thought the little mouse, fearing that this witch would cast another horrible spell.

"If it is not convenient, don't worry. I will fly on - it's no problem," added Bernice, noticing the mouse's worried look and her little mouth hanging open with shock.

But Mousey Mousey was such a kind little mouse that she felt bad about sending the witch away, and Bernice did not look as mean as her mother, Agatha. There was no wart on her little pert nose and she even wore a tiny pair of PINK studs in her ears.

"No, you can't fly on when you are tired," said Mousey Mousey. "Please come in and have a rest. You can have some tea and biscuits with me, but I haven't got any of the bat wing biscuits or spider leg cheese straws that your mother likes."

"Thank goodness for that," giggled Bernice. She took out her magic wand, waved it twice and said a spell to make herself small enough to follow the mouse into the cottage. As Bernice sat in a dark armchair she noticed Mousey Mousey had tears in her eyes.

"What is the matter?" asked the young witch.

Mousey Mousey looked up and wailed: "My cottage used to be pretty and all my things were pink. Your mother turned them black and purple and left spiders on the walls. She even complained about my tea and my home-made biscuits."

Feeling braver than ever before, the mouse added: "I hope you have not come to make my cottage even worse."

"No, no," said the witch. "I quite like pink." As she spoke she touched her tiny pink stud earrings and pulled back her coat to reveal pink satin high-heeled boots.

"Not too much, of course, but just a touch of pink is nice - and it drives my mother mad."

Bernice said this with a little smile on her face, but, after looking round at all the dark furniture and curtains, her expression changed to one of sadness.

Mousey Mousey brought in tea and biscuits and the young witch thanked her.

"You have a nice home and I agree that it could do with some bright things in it. We younger witches have lots of new ideas and do not always stick to the old ways.

"The older witches like everything to be black - you were lucky to get purple cushions! The trouble is that once a witch has cast a spell it is very hard to change it, and something always remains."

Bernice drank her tea and told Mousey Mousey of her adventures. How one day her broomstick disappeared and she finally found it had been taken by a naughty goblin. He was just about to chop it up for firewood, when she saw him. "I made the goblin hopping mad by turning him into a frog for an hour," she said with a broad smile.

Another time when she and her best friend Verity were on their way to a new evening class and got lost, they ended up in the Land of the Hook Nosed Giants. Bernice recalled: "The giants chased us and nearly caught us, but I quickly cast a spell which turned one of them into a parrot. The other giants ran away in case I changed them into parrots, too." This made Mousey Mousey laugh.

"Well," said Bernice. "I must be going, but thank you for the tea and LOVELY biscuits - perhaps I could call again one day and see how you are, and I will bring you some of my pink things which will NOT turn black."

Mousey Mousey thanked Bernice and walked with her down the garden path before waving her goodbye.

Not all witches were bad, she decided, and an occasional visit from Bernice would be nice as she did enjoy hearing about her adventures - especially the story about turning a nasty giant into a parrot.

So Mousey Mousey was feeling a little better as she went back inside her cottage, shutting the front door behind her, but suddenly there was a BANG and a WIZZ and something magical happened.

Little STARS started to fly around each room, and with a PING-PING-PING everything they touched turned PINK. At first the 'pings' frightened

Mousey Mousey, and she hid under the table, but soon she was delighted.

PING - her curtains turned pink; PING - her carpets changed back to pink; PING - her cushions became pink once more. As, everything in her cottage turned pink, the little mouse hopped about, clapping her hands in glee.

Her trust and kindness in letting another witch into her home had been rewarded.

She felt warm and happy because her little cottage was once again all pink.

The delighted mouse ran out and stood by the river, straining her eyes to see if Bernice was still visible, and in the distance she could just make out a little dot in the sky. Mousey Mousey shouted: "THANK YOU BERNICE, THANK YOU. Please come back sometime and have tea and biscuits with me again, and I'll make some cake with lots of pink icing."

But the mouse wondered what Bernice had meant when she said that once a witch had cast a spell something always remained.

She went inside her beautiful pink cottage, and as she closed the door six BRIGHT PINK spiders scuttled under an armchair.

Mousey Mousey couldn't help laughing.

Kidnapped by a Big Green Parrot

Kidnapped by a Big Green Parrot

Mousey Mousey sat on her doorstep cleaning her little pink shoes, thinking of the strange things that had been appearing around her cottage.

Two weeks ago she noticed that there were great big bird footprints all over her garden. Then, a couple of days later, as she swept cobwebs out of the corner of her kitchen, and shooed six little pink spiders out of the front door, she noticed a large green feather on the carpet. 'Where could that have come from?' she thought.

The very next morning two more green feathers appeared, one by the riverbank and the other in her garden. Perhaps the one on her carpet had been blown in by the wind, but that still did not explain the footprints. Why was a big green bird coming into her garden?

As Mousey Mousey cleaned her shoes, two pink spiders scuttled by her, trying to get back into the cottage. 'Drat these spiders,' thought the little mouse. They had been running around her cottage ever since the visit of that nasty witch Agatha, who had turned all her lovely pink things black and filled the cottage with spiders and cobwebs.

Fortunately, Agatha's daughter Bernice had changed everything back to pink. She could not completely cancel her mother's spell, and the spiders remained, but at least they had turned pink.

Bernice and Mousey Mousey had become good friends - they laughed at the same things and Bernice loved the biscuits and cakes that the little mouse made.

Unlike her Mother, Bernice liked the colour pink. She wore bright pink boots and pink ear studs, and the last time she visited she also had a pink streak in her hair.

Mousey Mousey had pink hair on the top of her head, too, as well as a little pink nose and pink whiskers.

As her shoes were now beautifully clean, she stood up and was about to go inside her cottage when she spotted another feather and huge footprints on her lawn. Mousey Mousey walked over to pick up the feather, but, before she could do so, a great green bird suddenly flew down. Within seconds he was standing menacingly in front of her.

Mousey Mousey screamed because she had never seen a bird this big before. He looked very cross and shouted: "I bet you think I am a parrot, but I'm NOT." He scratched the ground and squawked as he said this.

"My name is BOGMAS and I'm really a GIANT. Your friend Bernice, the witch, turned me into this ugly bird, and I have been trying to find her to get my REVENGE." He gave another loud squawk and pulled out a feather. "These horrible feathers itch so much sometimes that I tear them out."

"How dreadful for you," said Mousey Mousey.

"Yes, and it's all Bernice's fault," snapped Bogmas. "I have been flying around looking for that thoughtless witch. I finally saw her coming this way on her broomstick from the Black Mountains, so I tried to follow her. She flew very fast and I couldn't keep up, but twice I've seen Bernice leaving your cottage. I'm sure she will come back again. "I have a plan to catch her and make her sorry that she turned me into a parrot -

SQUAWK." Bogmas scratched the ground and tugged at another feather.

He suddenly walked right up to the mouse and tried to pick her up in his beak.

A startled Mousey Mousey dodged out of the way and ran for the door. She nearly managed to get into her cottage, but the parrot spread his massive wings in front of her and squawked: "Don't try that again, or I will get really cross. You are coming with me back to the Land of the Hook Nosed Giants. Your friend Bernice will see all these feathers in your garden and know I have been here. She will come to rescue you and I will be waiting for her - SQUAWK."

The parrot plucked out two more giant feathers and threw them on the doorstep.

Then, with a whoosh of his wings, he picked up the little mouse in his beak. She was frozen with fear as he soared into the air and flew back towards the village of the Hook Nosed Giants. He climbed higher and higher, with Mousey Mousey swinging from his strange-looking hooked beak. She was too frightened to scream or struggle as she did not want to be dropped from this height. It seemed like ages before finally the bird began to fly lower and landed in a valley.

There were huge old houses amongst the trees and Mousey Mousey could see giants with big, curved noses, walking about.

Bogmas dropped Mousey Mousey from his beak and chuckled as she rolled into some bramble bushes. The mouse hopped out quickly and rubbed her little hands, which were scratched. The parrot laughed again.

"Now we will wait for the witch," he said with a snarl before walking over to the nearest house and pushing Mousey Mousey inside.

A large grubby room contained two very big chairs, a table against the wall and a huge bed, which was pushed into a corner behind the door.

Another door opened and through it stepped a giant woman with black crooked teeth and odd eyes. One eye looked to the left and the other to the right.

"Why have you brought that mouse into our house, you old fool?" she demanded.

Bogmas retorted: "I told you I was going to find that rotten witch who turned me into a parrot - SQUAWK. I know she will come looking for this mouse, as they are friends, and when she does I will have her right in the middle of our village, where she will not escape. Then I will have my REVENGE."

Mousey Mousey remembered Bernice telling a story about how she had turned a giant into a parrot on one of her trips to the Black Mountains after he and his friends had chased her.

Bogmas sat down at the table and slammed down his wings. "Now where's my dinner, you squint-eyed hag?" he shouted. "Do I have to wait all day for it? - SQUAWK." The old woman, whose name was Snerj, went over to the cupboard and came back with a plate full of mouldy- looking bread, ham and cheese plus a glass of milk. Bogmas noisily gobbled down the food and drank the milk, wiping his beak on his sleeve and burping. He gave a big sigh before waddling over to lay on the bed in the corner. "Watch that mouse, old woman," he said. "Lock her in a cupboard or somewhere. If she disappears I will hold you responsible - SQUAWK!" He put his big head on the grubby pillow and went to sleep, snoring loudly.

Snerj looked over at Mousey Mousey with her squinty glare and then walked across the room to lock the door. She briefly went into the kitchen to fetch one of her largest saucepans, which she turned upside down and placed over the mouse.

Finally, she sat on top of the saucepan, and her wrinkled face creased into a soppy smile. "The mouse won't escape now," she muttered.

An hour passed and Mousey Mousey crouched in the dark, worried that she was unable to warn her friend Bernice. She knew there was nothing she could do while she was trapped under the saucepan, but she made plans should she be lucky enough to escape.

Snerj's eyes rolled in her head - she was so tired and once or twice caught herself slipping off the saucepan. Bogmas' snoring did not help as she battled to avoid falling asleep herself, but her eyelids kept slowly shutting over her glazed eyes.

A little snore escaped her crooked lips and she sprang upright trying to stay awake. A second hour passed and Snerj' could not stop herself snoring again. This time she failed to wake herself up and slid off the saucepan, upsetting it as she fell. The mouse quickly ran out from underneath the saucepan, jumped up onto the windowsill and through the window, which was slightly open.

Mousey Mousey's mind was racing. 'I must not stop until I find somewhere to hide', she thought. 'The Giants will hunt for me'.

So she ran and ran until she came across an old mouse hole under a gooseberry bush, tucked away from sight. She hoped that Bernice would come looking for her when she found Mousey Mousey's little cottage empty, and all those feathers scattered around the garden.

Bogmas woke with a loud snore and a squawk. He stretched his wings and started to clean his feathers before remembering that he was not a bird but a giant.

Standing up, Bogmas noticed his wife laying on the floor next to a large saucepan. He ignored her and looked for the mouse.

"WHERE'S THE MOUSE?" Bogmas yelled at his wife. "Where is she?"

Snerj jumped up immediately and shook her head, trying to clear the sleep from her crooked eyes. She suddenly spotted the upturned saucepan, yet managed to keep her voice claim. "Husband, I covered the mouse with the saucepan so she could not escape, but I fell off to sleep. She must be here somewhere. Don't worry - let's look," and she started searching under the bed and table.

When Snerj walked past the window she saw that it was slightly open – wide enough for a mouse to have climbed through! With a sneaky shout of "Is that her over there?" she caused Bogmas to look the other way while she closed the window. At least that was one less thing her husband could shout about.

"Where?" he demanded. "You must be seeing things." Bogmas and Snerj looked everywhere for the mouse, but she was not there. "WHAT HAS HAPPENED TO HER?" the angry parrot yelled, turning over furniture as he strutted around the shack, flapping his wings.

"Be careful, husband," said Snerj. "You might tread on her and then you will have no mouse to trap the witch." Suddenly Bogmas stood still as a thought seemed to strike him. He declared: "We may no longer have the mouse, but Bernice doesn't know that. Bernice will still come here trying to find her little friend."

This cheered Bogmas and he pranced around, stretching his wings. "I cannot stay here, wife. I must go out and fly as my wings are stiff, but I will be back in a little while. You keep watch - you may still find the mouse, SQUAWK!" With that he went out of the door and flew up into the sky. Snerj started to pick up the furniture that Bogmas had turned over. When she had finished she got on the bed and went back to sleep.

Mousey Mousey was snug and warm in her mouse hole under the gooseberry bush.

But after hiding there all day, she was getting hungry and wondered if it was safe to go outside as it was becoming dark.

She was still wearing her bright pink dress and apron and was worried that she would be easily seen. So she took them off and hid them under a large leaf. That gave Mousey Mousey an idea - if she covered herself with dark leaves no one would see her.

She carefully poked her head out of the hole and picked two large gooseberries. She then returned to the hole and squeezed the sticky juice out of the fruit, rubbing it onto her fur. She gathered up some leaves that were on the floor and stuck them on her back. Finally, after putting one on top of her head, she was suitably disguised and ready to leave the mouse hole.

Mousey Mousey walked to the edge of the wood and started to collect lots of stones. She put them together on a piece of open ground to spell out 'MOUSEY', hoping that Bernice would see the word as she flew over the village.

It shouldn't matter if Bogmas saw it, she thought, because he was an ignorant giant who probably could not read. After waiting all night without any sign of Bernice, the little mouse went back to her hole. She spent most of the next day checking where she had left the stones to make sure they were still there. She was just about to return to her hole when she saw a tiny black dot appear in the sky. It came closer and closer and then Mousey

Mousey could see that it was a witch flying on her broomstick.

Mousey Mousey took the leaves off her fur and waved her arms. She jumped up and down and finally the witch came close enough to see her. To the little mouse's great surprise it was not Bernice but Agatha, her mother - the naughty witch who had turned everything in Mousey Mousey's cottage black and purple the last time she had seen her. Mousey Mousey was about to run back under the trees, but it was too late, Agatha had spotted her. She swooped down and landed in front of the little mouse.

"Hello, Mousey Mousey. Do you remember me, I had tea with you once," she said in her scratchy old voice.

"Yes. Hello," replied the little mouse, not wanting to displease the old witch, as she knew what she was capable of doing.

"Lost, are you my dear? My, my, you look a mess - your fur is all sticky with gum. What has happened to you?" But just as Mousey Mousey was about to reply there was a great swooshing sound and the giant parrot flew down. He knocked the witch to the floor, snatching her wand and snapping her broomstick in two.

"You stupid parrot," croaked Agatha, as she stumbled to her feet. "How dare you take my wand and break my broomstick - do you realise who I am?"

"Oh, yes, SQUAWK, I know who you are," chuckled the excited Bogmas. "You are the witch who turned me into a parrot when I chased you, and I have been waiting to get my revenge. Now I shall have it."

The parrot had obviously mistaken Agatha for Bernice, her daughter, partly because the light was fading in the late afternoon and partly because he was just a silly old giant with a very small brain.

He laughed and squawked before pulling out another feather, enjoying the sight of the witch's discomfort. "Not so clever now, are you?" Bogmas chuckled.

Then a voice from behind him said: "Oh, I think I am much more clever than a stupid green parrot."

Bogmas spun round and before he knew what had hit him a shower of magic stars burst from Bernice's wand and struck him full in the chest. He bent over double and remained still, unable to move.

Mousey Mousey jumped for joy at seeing Bernice, and there was even a cackle from the old witch.

Bernice told her little friend that Agatha had seen the word 'MOUSEY' written in stone while flying overhead earlier in the day and had flown home to get her.

"I'm so grateful to you both for rescuing me," said Mousey Mousey.

"Don't mention it," Bernice replied. "Now we must go quickly, my friend, in case we are seen by the other giants." But Mousey Mousey was troubled and asked Bernice if she could take the spell off the parrot by turning him back to a giant.

"Have you gone mad?" Agatha asked.

The mouse explained: "I have learned that some people have never known kindness, and, although it does not always work, it is worth the effort to give them one chance to change their ways. Please let us try."

"You are a very kind mouse," Bernice said. "Alright, I'll do it if that is what you want."

She pointed her wand at the wretched Bogmas, who immediately started to move. He stretched his wings and glared at the witches and the little mouse.

Bernice told him: "My friend Mousey Mousey wants me to change you back into a giant. She thinks that you will be so pleased by this act of kindness that you will no longer be your wicked old self. I am not so sure that it will work, but I have promised her that we will try."

With that, the young witch waved her wand and the sparks once again covered Bogmas. PING, PING, PING - one by one the parrot feathers disappeared and there, standing before them, was the hook nosed giant.

Bogmas was so shocked he could not move. Then, slowly, a big smile lit up his face and he pranced about dancing in the moonlight.

The ground shook as he danced and clapped his hands. He looked so funny that Mousey Mousey laughed and even the witches smiled. Bogmas felt his arms and legs to make sure the feathers were gone. Then he stood still, breathing heavily, and stared at the three small figures in front of him.

Finally he spoke. "Thank you, thank you little mouse. I am a wicked giant and I cannot promise to mend ALL my old ways, but as you have changed me back I will try my best." As he said this his wife Snerj appeared and her mouth dropped open when she saw her husband.

Bogmas held out his hand and she took hold of it, smiling. "We must go now," said Bernice. "Don't forget, Bogmas you owe your appearance to this little mouse - maybe one day you can repay her kindness."

They watched as the giants walked away and Mousey Mousey noticed that Bogmas still had one large feather sticking out of the back of his head. She remembered Bernice telling her that magic was hard to reverse, and something always remained.

"Come, mother, let us take Mousey Mousey back to her cottage and go home," said Bernice. "You had both better get on my broomstick as yours is broken in two."

Agatha picked up the pieces of her own broomstick and climbed on behind Bernice. Mousey Mousey squeezed between them.

As Bernice kicked off from the ground Mousey Mousey noticed that she was wearing black boots, not her usual bright pink ones. 'Was this a gesture she had made to her mother in return for helping rescue me?' she wondered. But when she looked up she saw that Bernice was still wearing her little pink earrings, and a pink streak remained in her hair.

It was then that Mousey Mousey remembered her little dress and apron which she had left under the leaves in the old mouse hole. Well, never mind, she was warm enough in her underwear.

Mousey Mousey was just so pleased to be going home that it did not bother her - and there were plenty more aprons and dresses in her cupboard!

As they climbed higher in the sky, Mousey Mousey looked down and shouted one last "Good-bye" to the two giants, who were standing waving farewell to them.

When they reached Mousey Mousey's cottage, the witches started to say their good-byes.

"Please have some tea before you go," Mousey Mousey pleaded.

"NO," insisted Agatha. "We must get home to Witchy Poo Corner as it is late and my old bones are not as young as they used to be. Besides, I have a potion in the shed that needs stirring."

"Thank you very much, my friends," said Mousey Mousey. "I'll never forget your kindness in rescuing me or the happy smiles on the faces of Bogmas and his wife when they waved us good-bye." She blew them both a kiss as they prepared to fly off on Bernice's broomstick. Agatha obviously hated kisses and screwed up her nose, which caused Bernice to laugh out loud at her mother.

'Oh, what an adventure,' thought Mousey Mousey, closing her little pink door and glancing inside her cottage. All her things were still pink. 'What a relief,' she thought - then she spotted five little spiders scuttling by, followed by one black one.

Obviously Agatha could not resist meddling, but fortunately she had left everything else pink.

The Village Fête

The Village Fête

It was the day of the village fête and Mousey Mousey was very excited. She had been making cakes all week and had just finished taking them to her stall.

Suddenly there was a loud knock on the door of her cottage, and Mousey Mousey thought one of her friends had come to call. As she opened the door she was surprised to see Agatha, the witch, holding a large rusty cauldron.

"Hello, dear," said the witch. "I heard you are having a fête and I thought you would like this."

The mouse was deeply worried as the last time Agatha had come into her cottage she had turned nearly everything black with one of her naughty spells.

"Hold on a minute, dear," shouted Agatha. "I'll never get through the door - just let me find my wand so that I can reduce my size."

She poked about in her pocket and produced an old bent wand which she waved in the air. Immediately the old witch and the cauldron shrunk sufficiently to get into the cottage.

"Ah, that's better, dear - out of the way, now," said Agatha, as she shoved past Mousey Mousey and PLONKED the cauldron down on the pink carpet. "There, dear. I'm never going to use this old thing again, as I've got several other pots to create my spells in. So now it can be sold at your village fête."

The mouse looked at the rusty old cauldron, and wondered who on earth would buy such a thing - no one in Dobble, she was sure. But, remembering her manners, she said: "Thank you. That was very nice of you.

"Now where can we put it?"

Mousey Mousey had already noticed some rust on her pretty pink hall carpet and wanted to get the cauldron outside as quickly as possible. "Perhaps you could take it into the back garden and put it in the shed," she suggested. "Oh, you have a SHED, dear," replied Agatha. "How wonderful. I have a shed at home and I do all sorts in it. I have four cauldrons bubbling away with potions, and at this very moment Bernice is stirring them for me.

"It was vital someone stay behind to keep an eye on things. I insisted on coming here myself because, as well as the cauldron, I wanted to bring you some tasty CRUNCHY BAT WING BISCUITS AND SPIDER LEG CHEESE STRAWS.

"We love them, so I thought they could be sold at the fête." The witch cackled as she said this and Mousey Mousey wondered whether she was up to her mischief again.

"I have bought several pots of HAIRY LEG CREAM, too, and it works a treat, dear.

"I never have cold legs in the winter. LOOK!" She pulled up her black robe to proudly show Mousey Mousey two very black hairy legs.

The mouse stared, not knowing what to say, and pretended to cough.

"Oh dear, got a little cough have we?" questioned the witch. "I have the very thing brewing in my shed, EARWIG SYRUP - it wriggles its way right down into your chest and gets rid of all that nasty stuff that gathers there."

The witch picked up the cauldron, inside of which were her own versions of biscuits and cheese straws, and carried it out to the garden shed.

Mousey Mousey went into the kitchen to fetch a pan and brush to get the rust off her pink carpet. When Agatha came back the mouse was bending down brushing the carpet. "Oh dear, have I made a mess? Never mind - leave it to me," said the witch, taking out her wand and giving it a little wave.

PING - the rust disappeared instantly. "There, all gone," laughed Agatha. "No need to thank me, dear."

Mousey Mousey went into the kitchen and brought back some cakes on a plate.

"Would you like one or two of these?" she asked.

"Yes," said the witch. "But I'll just sprinkle some spiders legs on them" - and so she did, all over the pink icing! "I'LL make the tea this time," she added, pushing past Mousey Mousey again to go into the kitchen.

"Where are the cups, dear?" called the witch, crashing around.

Mousey Mousey rushed into the kitchen, fearing that all her pretty cups would be smashed. "W... w...wait I'll get them for you," she stammered, reaching inside one of the cupboards and taking out the oldest china, while pushing her new pink tea-set further back.

The witch continued looking for the tea-pot, opening and closing the cupboards noisily.

"Here it is," said Mousey Mousey, taking out a pink tea- pot. She only had one, so she hoped the witch would not break it as she popped in 10 teaspoons of tea as Agatha liked.

Agatha went into the living-room and, after drinking the tea and eating some cakes laced with spiders' legs, she reached into her pocket.

Mousey Mousey thought she was trying to find her wand, but the witch pulled out her sun-glasses and put them on over her nose, fitting them around her large wart. "That's better - I hate all this pink," she said. "Now, would you like me to tell your fortune from the tea-leaves, dear?"

"Well, I'm not sure, really," answered the mouse. "If it's bad news I shall only worry and if it's..."

"Don't be silly, dear - let's see." With that Agatha turned the cup over and stared at the leaves. "Tut-tut," gasped the witch.

"What is it?" whispered the anxious mouse, her pink hair beginning to stand up on her head in alarm.

"Oh, nothing much - it seems there may be a few little problems to sort out today."

"Do you mean at the fête?" asked the worried mouse. "Will there be problems at the fête?"

"Maybe," replied the witch, grinning in a mischievous manner. "The tea leaves won't give me a clear picture, but I'm sure there's nothing for you to worry your little head about.

"Well, I must go now. Bernice and I will be back this afternoon, and we would like to have our own stall to sell our potions and special knick-knacks. I'm sure they will be popular with your friends. So we will see you later." The witch walked to the door, went outside, changed into her normal size and got on her brand new broomstick. "Bye, dear," she called.

Mousey Mousey rushed back into her living room and looked around expecting to see her things had turned black, but luckily nothing had been changed - everything was still different shades of pretty pink, and her little pink hair-dryer sat in its usual place on the bedroom table.

As she went to wash up the tea things, there was another knock at the front door.

Mousey Mousey froze in fear, thinking the witch had come back for some reason.

"Hello," said a friendly voice when she opened the door. It was the portly figure of Ben Badger with a tray of plants in his hands. "Here are the plants you wanted for your garden - I thought I would bring them over early, as I have lots more to take to the fête."

"Thank you, Ben. They are lovely," Mousey Mousey replied as she took the tray.

Ben, peering over his spectacles, noticed that there were tears in her eyes, and asked: "What is the matter, little mouse? Why are you crying?"

Mousey Mousey took out her handkerchief and blew her nose. "Oh, Ben, do you remember the witch Agatha, who turned all my things black? Well, she is coming to the fête with Bernice, her daughter.

"She has been here to drop off a cauldron to sell, and said they want to have a stall. I am so frightened that she is going to do something awful."

Ben put his arm around his friend and said: "Don't worry, Mousey Mousey. We will all be there this time, and you said that Bernice is a friend, so she will not let Agatha play any of her tricks, I'm sure."

Mousey Mousey still looked worried. She told him: "Agatha predicted that there may be some problems today when she read my tea leaves. We must be careful not to upset her or she might ruin the fête."

An hour before the fête was due to open everyone was setting out their stalls. Mousey Mousey's stall was next to Ben's - she had baked tea cakes and iced buns, chocolate éclairs and biscuits. "They look good enough to eat," joked Ben.

"I should hope so," smiled Mousey Mousey. "Your plants look lovely, too, Ben."

Rachel came over to speak to the badger. "Can Billy help you today Ben?" she asked.

Billy was Rachel's oldest bunny and a very good, helpful rabbit.

"Yes, I would like that," said Ben, adjusting his spectacles. "I wish all my young bunnies were as good as Billy," sighed Rachel, causing her large front teeth to click together. "He and his sister Gabby are no trouble at all. Gabby loves helping with the little ones and has lots of patience, even when they hide her things.

"Trudy and Ashlee are always running around getting into mischief. The baby thinks they are so funny and tries to copy them. I hope they do not get into any trouble at the fête."

"Just tell them to keep away from the old witch Agatha when she arrives," warned Mousey Mousey. "We don't want her to get upset and cast any of her spells, do we?" Villagers were soon flocking to the fête as it was a lovely sunny day, and Mousey Mousey's cakes proved very popular.

Four hungry squirrels bought lots of cupcakes and two families of hamsters were quick to purchase some of the bigger ones.

It did not take long for the little mouse to sell everything on her stall. This meant she could go with Rachel to watch as young Gabby had her face painted by Molly Mole.

The little bunny shared Mousey Mousey's love of pink so Molly gave her some pink whiskers and a pink nose. There was still no sign of the witches and Mousey Mousey began to wonder if they were going to come at all. Then suddenly two shadows appeared in the sky.

Making themselves smaller, the witches flew down and landed a few yards from Molly's stall. As usual, Bernice did not wear a hat and her long hair shone in the sunlight - as did her short pink cape!

"Hello, Mousey Mousey," called Bernice. "Do you like my new cape? I can turn it round when I get home so none of the other witches will know one side is pink."

She showed her friend the inside of it, which was black, and grinned broadly - until she turned to look at her mother, who was scowling.

"I hate pink," snapped Agatha, feeling in her pocket for her sunglasses.

The old hag then took out her wand, but did not point it at Bernice's cape. Instead, sparks flew from the wand and PING - a table appeared with a rusty cauldron standing in the middle of it. The cauldron was the one Agatha had put in Mousey Mousey's shed.

Agatha started laying out all the things that she had bought with her - including some black books with rather weird titles like Spells for Dummies, 101 ways to cook spiders, Brew your own Frog's Juice, Extraordinary Uses for Toe Clippings and How to do just about anything with Ear Wax. She also had several half-melted candles, a very old knitted hat with two holes in it and a pair of black shoes with pointy toes.

Agatha waved her wand again and several jars of creams and potions appeared on the table.

"Mother, what have you brought with you?" laughed Bernice as she arranged her own things on the stall.

"Stop annoying me, Bernice," grumbled Agatha. "I am trying my best for you, dear - trying to meet all your friends, just like a good mother should."

Mousey Mousey was shocked. Perhaps she had been too hard on Agatha - after all, the old witch had helped save the little mouse from the big green parrot.

Suddenly Agatha began shouting to passers-by. "Come and look at these wonderful things everyone." The villagers were also attracted by the witches' costumes, which they thought were fancy dress.

Several of them bought earrings and fancy combs from Bernice, but nobody wanted Agatha's books, candles, old hat and shoes. Not surprisingly,

Mousey Mousey and her friends passed up the chance to taste Agatha's crunchy bat wing biscuits and spider leg cheese straws,

"I'm going to take a walk around the fête, dear, as no one is buying my things," the old witch moaned to Bernice. "I can't understand it – I thought my spider leg cheese straws would sell like hot cakes."

Agatha stopped at Molly's stall where face-painting was proving very popular. One of the youngsters waiting to be painted, a very excited little squirrel, pointed at Agatha and shouted: "I WANT TO LOOK LIKE HER."

Far from being annoyed, the witch seemed to be flattered and asked Molly: "Would you like me to sit with you, dear, so that you can copy my face?"

"Oh, thank you, Agatha," said Molly. "Sit there and I'll begin."

The witch smiled as she sat and watched the young squirrel having her face painted. She touched her wand in her pocket and mumbled something under her breath. Agatha could not stop a cackle escaping from her mouth and Molly turned to look at her. "Are you alright, Agatha?" she asked, alarmed by the dreadful noise.

"Yes, dear," replied the witch. "Make sure you use plenty of black paint on her lips and round her eyes so that this child looks just like me." Agatha knew that her spell would cause the paint to stay on for several days. Oh, this was such fun!

The chuckling old witch went back to her stall and picked up the black shoes. "I'm just going to see if someone would like these shoes as a gift, dear," said Agatha to Bernice. Mousey Mousey watched Agatha stride off with the shoes and felt a little prickling down her neck. The old witch was being really nice to everyone today, but the worried mouse could not help wondering if she could be trusted.

Agatha took the shoes over to Ben's stall. "I can't sell these shoes, Ben, so I thought you could have them for gardening," she told him.

"That's very kind of you, Agatha - I hope they are my size. I'll try them on to see if they fit," he replied with a broad smile.

The witch touched her wand and Ben found the shoes fitted perfectly. As he walked up and down in them Agatha giggled and wiped a tear from her eye. She knew that the shoes would not come off Ben's feet for two days, and they would get tighter and tighter. "Oh, I love being naughty," she chuckled.

She returned to her stall and picked up the hat, which she took over to Rachel Rabbit.

"Rachel, dear, I have the very thing for you here," she announced. "Look - this hat has holes in it for your ears, and will keep you warm in the winter."

Rachel thanked Agatha and tried the hat on. It was a bit tight, but she did not want to upset the witch, so she did not remove it.

Agatha bit her lip to prevent herself laughing. She had put a spell on the hat, too, and, just like Ben's shoes, it would not come off for two days. During that time it would squeeze Rachel's head as it got tighter.

Oh, she would have to come again next year - she had not realised that fêtes could be such fun. Her sides were splitting - what could she do next? Oh, yes, that little mouse who liked everything pink would be an ideal person to play another trick on.

She went back to her stall and filled a bottle with water from a jug, took out her wand and waved it over the bottle, turning the water pink. She put a label on the bottle, naming it 'Delicious Surprise Lotion'.

Agatha then went over to Molly's stall, where Mousey Mousey and Bernice were sitting talking to their friends. "Hello, dears, what a lovely day we have had," Agatha began. "But I noticed that your ears are getting burnt in this sun, so I thought you would like some of my sun- lotion to rub on them."

"That's very thoughtful of you," said Molly.

"Yes," added Mousey Mousey. "It has been so sunny that my nose feels quite hot."

"This is just the thing," Agatha assured them, taking out the bottle from her pocket.

She held out the lotion and was just unscrewing the cap on the bottle when two of Rachel Rabbit's youngsters, Ashlee and Trudy, suddenly appeared. They were enjoying a great game of tag and were running too fast to stop.

The two bunnies did not see the witch until it was too late, and could not prevent themselves bumping into her. Agatha's hat fell off and the lotion flew up into the air.

The liquid came out of the bottle and landed right in the middle of the old witch's head.

Rachel Rabbit was horrified. She howled: "I'm so sorry, Agatha. You NAUGHTY bunnies - just you wait till I get you home! You are both going on the naughty step."

Ashlee and Trudy did not wait to hear any more – they ran off to hide.

Molly Mole picked up a cloth from her stall and began to wipe off the liquid from the witch's head, but only succeeded in spreading it all over her hair.

To her amazement Agatha's hair started to turn bright PINK.

"W-w-w-ould you like me to wash your hair, Agatha?" stammered Molly, as she glanced over at Mousey Mousey and her other friends, who were also staring at the witch's head in disbelief.

"NO I WOULD NOT," fumed Agatha. Then she called across to her daughter: "BERNICE, BERNICE - get your things together, dear, we are going now."

Bernice came over to her mother and was just about to ask her why they were leaving, when she saw the bright pink hair on the witch's head. A small drop of the spilt lotion had turned the hairs on Agatha's large wart pink as well. "WHAT ARE YOU STARING AT?" spat Agatha. Bernice tried to keep her face straight, but had to turn her back to her mother for a few moments, as she struggled to stop herself from laughing out loud.

"Mother, what have you done to your hair?" asked Bernice when she turned and looked at her. "It's...PINK."

"W-H-A-T?" shrieked Agatha as she ran around holding her head. She reached into her pocket and brought out her wand. "MIRROR," she shouted, and instantly a mirror appeared. "AHHHHH," screamed the witch at the sight of her bright pink hair and wart.

She picked up her hat and crammed it down over her head, but still some of her hair peaked out from underneath it.

"I must go home NOW, dear," she yelled at Bernice and ran for her broomstick.

Within seconds she was high in the sky, hanging on to her hat, heading for their home at Witchy Poo Corner. Everyone, including Bernice, stood looking up at the sky as the witch disappeared.

Ben groaned as he rubbed his sore feet. "These shoes your mother gave me are so tight I can't get them off," he told Bernice.

"That's strange," said Rachel. "This hat your mother gave me is getting tighter, too."

Bernice waved her wand and the shoes dropped off. She twirled it again and the hat fell off the rabbit's head.

"Oh, thank you, Bernice," they said. Next it was the turn of the young squirrel to have the black paint on her lips and around her eyes changed to normal paint.

Molly Mole came forward to ask: "Why is your mother always causing mischief? This time she seems to have been taught a lesson."

Bernice sighed, but had to smile when she remembered the colour of her mother's hair.

Later that evening Bernice and her friends sat in Mousey Mousey's cottage, eating cake, drinking tea and talking about Agatha.

Bernice explained that her mother would not be able to remove all of the spell that had turned her hair pink, because something always remained.

Mousey Mousey said: "My father used to tell me 'What goes around comes around'."

Bernice admitted: "Yes, my mother probably got what she deserves. And it's a lesson she will never forget because pink hair is her worst nightmare." They all roared with laughter.

Mousey Mousey in cliff-top drama

Mousey Mousey in cliff-top drama

It was just after eight o'clock on a sunny morning when Mousey Mousey's doorbell rang.

"Hello," called a deep voice. She opened the door to find Ben Badger standing there with his usual big smile. "Are you ready?" he asked.

"Yes, just let me get my bag, Ben." she replied. "It's perfect weather for a day trip to the seaside, isn't it?"

"Yes, Molly and I are really looking forward to it. What have you got in here?" he enquired as he took her bag. "It's quite heavy."

"A packed lunch with lots of my freshly baked scones, a couple of towels and some flip flops. Oh, and plenty of sun cream."

As they approached the coach Mousey Mousey could see her friends Molly Mole and Rachael

Rabbit waving at her through a window. Rachael Rabbit was holding on to her baby Sam, watching her other children, Trudy, Ashlee and Gabby, settling in their seats.

"Sorry, I hope I haven't kept you waiting," said Mousey Mousey.

The driver, Lenny, took her case, while Ben helped her on to the coach, where she found a seat two rows behind Ben and Molly. Rachael and her children were all sitting along the back row.

"Can I go and sit next to Mousey Mousey?" Gabby asked her Mum.

"Yes, if that is alright with her, but be good."

"I will Mum," said the little rabbit, hurrying to the front to ask Mousey Mousey.

"Yes, of course, Gabby, I would love to have your company." The thoughtful mouse patted the seat beside her, and asked: "Would you like to sit at the window?"

"Yes please."

"Hello everyone," came a loud voice over the intercom. "I am your driver Lenny. I hope you enjoy this trip to Shell Bay with Away Day coaches. I will be speaking to you over the intercom from time to time to tell you about interesting places we are passing through. So if everyone is ready we'll depart. Are you ready?"

"Yes we are," shouted Sally Squirrel, Harriet Hedgehog and Freddie Fox who were sitting near the back with their mums and dads.

"Then off we go!" The driver started the engine, revved it up a few times and the bright red coach trundled down the lane, beginning its journey to Shell Bay.

"I wish Billy and Tom could have come with us today," said Gabby, "but they are busy laying a new lawn for Mrs. Hare. I've been so looking forward to this."

Two hours later the coast came into view.

"Oh look, there's the sea!" yelled Gabby, excitedly. She stood up and called back to her mother. "We're almost there."

Everyone cheered as the little old coach rounded the bend and went down a steep hill towards the sea. Molly Mole started to sing "Oh I do like to be beside the seaside."

Soon they were all spread out on the beach. Ben and Molly hired a large umbrella so they could sit in the shade, and invited Mousey Mousey to join them under it.

"Oh, this is so lovely," said Mousey Mousey. "Blue sea and sky, a lovely breeze and delicious tasty scones covered with strawberry jam."

"Yes, your scones are the best," declared Molly, between mouthfuls.

Rachael was busy making sure the young rabbits had lots of sun cream on their noses and inside their long ears.

"Do we have to be covered in all this cream?" protested Ashlee, trying to pull away.

"Yes, you do," insisted his Mum. "It is so hot today and if you get sun burnt you'll be ill."

The little rabbits scampered off to have a paddle and then made themselves a huge sandcastle with a moat round it. The girls did most of the work, filling their buckets with water to empty into it.

Sam giggled as he wet his toes in the moat.

"Who'd like some tea?" asked Mousey Mousey as she opened a large flask.

"Yes please," Ben, Molly and Rachael replied.

"I love Shell Bay," said Ben. "I can remember coming here when I was little with my Mum and Dad. There were lots of caves to explore. It was such an adventure as they were always cold and dark. My Dad used to say that there was a witch living in one of them."

"We've had enough of witches," Molly told him.

"Except for Bernice - she has been so kind to me," said Mousey Mousey. "It's such a pity her mother is always causing trouble."

"Yes, my feet are still sore from those gardening shoes Agatha gave me," moaned Ben.

"It was so naughty of her making them get tighter and tighter," said Mousey Mousey. "But one of

Agatha's spells backfired, of course. Bernice says her mother still has three pink curls on her head."

"Serves her right!" declared Molly, and they all laughed.

Everyone enjoyed their day by the sea, but it was soon time for them to pack up and return home to Dobble.

The little rabbits gathered their buckets and spades. Rachael picked up Sam, who had fallen asleep, and they all went back to the coach.

"Can we come again?" asked Ashlee. "Can we, Mum, please?"

"Yes, I'm sure we can, and maybe next time Daddy will join us. He is so busy working these days as we have a lot of little mouths to feed. But he will be very pleased that you have each found a lovely shell to take home to him." "We're going to paint them different colours when we get home and put his name on them," said Trudy.

Lenny helped his passengers onto the coach and made an announcement over the intercom before starting up the engine.

"Hello everyone, did you all have a great time?"

"Yes we did," they all chorused.

"Well, I have a surprise for you. We're going back another way, along the Rolling Hills. I want you to see the pretty lights that come on at night in the villages below, and there will be fireworks, too, because the villagers are holding their annual festival. So you can all sit back and enjoy yourselves."

"Hooray!" everyone shouted.

The coach took a detour along the hilly route. Soon they could see lights twinkling in the little villages they passed. After about an hour the old coach started to splutter as it climbed to the top of a very steep hill where they could overlook the firework display. Lenny parked on a slope, several yards from the edge of a cliff, and put on the handbrake.

As it was quite cold he suggested that everyone stay on the coach to watch, but he peered out from the open door. Eventually the display started and the youngsters shouted in delight. Soon the sky lit up with blue, red, yellow and white fireworks, some bursting into showers and others into stars. Little Sam had woken up and was excitedly clapping his hands.

When the rockets took off and exploded into the darkening sky, most of the passengers moved towards the front of the coach to get a better view. At first nobody noticed as the vehicle slowly started to slip forward, but, as it gathered speed, Lenny was thrown out of the open door.

The coach hurtled closer to the cliff edge. Ben tried desperately to get into the driver's seat and put on the brake but was thrown backwards. Everyone began to scream. Mousey Mousey and Rachael desperately held on to the bunnies while all about them passengers toppled off balance.

"Help, help!" shouted a horrified Mousey Mousey as the front of the coach went over the cliff. Down and down it toppled towards the rocks below.

Suddenly the coach came to an abrupt halt and was pulled backwards by what seemed to be a huge hand. A large pair of eyes then peered through the windows at the terrified passengers. Mousey

Mousey could see a green feather waving about in the wind as they were transported back to the top of the cliff. The hand held the little red coach firmly and within minutes had laid it to rest on the side of the road.

As everyone got to their feet and staggered off the coach, a towering figure loomed over them and a booming voice said: "Hello Mousey Mousey."

It was Bogmas, the giant who'd once been turned into a parrot by Bernice. He still had a single green feather sticking out of his head.

"Hel...lo," stuttered Mousey Mousey.

Bogmas looked down at her and grinned. "I was watching the firework display with my wife Snerj when I saw your coach slide towards the cliff top edge and start to topple over. I thought you would appreciate a lift." He laughed out loud at his own joke as the passengers stared at him in disbelief, still too shocked to say anything. "It's lucky for you that I was here or you and your friends would have all crashed on to the rocks below."

"Thank you so much, Bogmas. You saved our lives," gasped Mousey Mousey, suddenly finding her voice and wiping the sweat from her brow.

"Think nothing of it," beamed Bogmas. "You persuaded that witch to turn me back into a giant when she was going to leave me as a huge, ugly parrot for the rest of my life. So one good turn deserves another."

MESSAGE FROM THE AUTHOR ABOUT MORE ADVENTURES

I hope you enjoyed reading my Mousey Mousey stories as much as I did writing them.

You can read more about her in MOUSEY MOUSEY AND THE WITCHES' REVENGE, which also contains further fun adventures about Agatha and all of Mousey Mousey's friends.

Read on to see tasters of this second Mousey Mousey book plus GIANT STICKER MONSTER AND OTHER CHILDREN'S STORIES – as well as details about THE SECRET POTION, recommended for Harry Potter fans by actress June Whitfield.

If you would like more stories after that, I need some help from you. Would you please ask your Mum to go to Amazon and Goodreads and give a review, telling other people what you think about one (or more) or these books?

Reviews are so important - they encourage other people to enjoy them, too, which means we can bring you more adventures!

BYEEE, HEATHER FLOOD

READ ON TO SEE

THE START OF THE NEXT

MOUSEY MOUSEY BOOK...

MOUSEY MOUSEY AND THE WITCHES' REVENGE

Chapter 1

"Hurry up, Dad," called Ashlee Rabbit as he ran towards Mousey Mousey's cottage, with his two sisters Gabby and Trudy.

The magical village of Dobble was covered in crispy, crunchy snow and the three little rabbits giggled as they threw snowballs at their father Daniel and big brother Billy.

It was very windy and their mother Rachel was having trouble keeping up with them all, as she was pushing baby Sam in his buggy.

Gabby ran ahead and knocked on Mousey Mousey's door.

"Hello everyone, Merry Christmas," smiled Mousey Mousey, welcoming the friends she had invited for Christmas dinner to her cottage.

Gabby, Ashlee and Trudy were so excited as Billy laid the presents they had brought under the Christmas tree after exchanging greetings with Molly Mole and Ben Badger, who had already arrived and were sitting in the living room.

A CRACK of thunder suddenly sounded near the cottage. "I think we are in for a bad storm," said Daniel Rabbit, brushing snow off his trousers.

"I agree," replied Ben. "The wind has been howling all morning. I had to rescue a little polecat who had been blown over in the lane earlier."

"Mmm, that looks good," interrupted Rachel as she strode into the living room. The table was set with red and gold Christmas crackers, and an enormous trifle was sitting in the middle.

Another CRACK of thunder shook the cottage, making Mousey Mousey jump.

"Look at the green lightning," shouted Ashlee, running to the window with Gabby.

"Yes, it's awful," replied Mousey Mousey. "Thank goodness you all got here safely – but where's your brother Tom?"

"He couldn't come – he's snowed in," said Trudy. "He's been working on a farm where the snow is even deeper than it is here."

"Can we open the presents?" asked Ashlee excitedly. Mousey Mousey chuckled. "Christmas dinner first," she said.

"Yes, it's time to eat," added Ben, rubbing his ample tummy.

They all sat around the large table, apart from baby Sam, who was asleep in his little rocking chair as he had already been fed. He was dressed in a red Father Christmas suit, and his little rabbit ears poked out of the hat.

"Shall we pull the crackers?" asked Gabby, but before anyone could answer there was knock at the front door.

"Who could this be?" said Mousey Mousey, peering out of the curtains. "I am not expecting anyone else for dinner."

"Hurry up!" demanded the mischievous witch Agatha.

Will Agatha spoil Christmas for everyone? Will the storm wreck their homes? What happens when Agatha clashes with her worst enemy? Find out by reading the rest of this story and others in Mousey Mousey and the Witches' Revenge!

YOU CAN NOW ENJOY

A TASTER FROM

GIANT STICKER MONSTER

AND OTHER

CHILDREN'S STORIES...

GIANT STICKER MONSTER AND OTHER CHILDREN'S STORIES

Once upon a time there was a GIANT STICKER MONSTER, whose name was GIANT STICKER MONSTER, of course.

He was simply enormous and used to walk backwards and forwards in his GIANT STICKER MONSTER boots, looking for things – and people - to stick his stickers on.

He had no friends because he was without doubt the most annoying creature in the whole wide world. But he didn't seem to mind, and was happy enough listening to music on his headphones.

One day while the GIANT STICKER MONSTER was trudging around in the winter snow, he noticed this little black and white dog looking at him through a garden gate.

"WOOF, WOOF," barked the dog, and immediately the GIANT STICKER MONSTER placed a sticker over the poor animal's mouth.

The GIANT STICKER MONSTER laughed as the dog tried in vain to bark again, and carried on walking through the snow, looking to cause more mischief.

When he came to a school he rubbed his hands with glee at the thought of being able to find some more victims.

He hid behind a clump of trees and when the children came out he ran up to them, shouted 'BOO!' and stuck a sticker on each one.

Some of the girls shrieked as he stuck them in their hair, and the boys shouted at him angrily as he placed stickers on their noses. The mischievous GIANT STICKER MONSTER simply ran off giggling. Wasn't he naughty?

Oh, what will that naughty Giant Sticker Monster do next? Head to the zoo? Oh no, what terrible tricks will he play on the poor animals? And what happens if he meets with Father Christmas?

Find out, and read the other brilliant stories that delight children everywhere in *Giant Sticker Monster and Other Children's Stories* - there are lovely tales about The Naughty Kitten, The Happy Snowman, Maurice the Mischievous Donkey, The Lonely King and more!

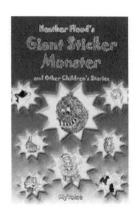

ABOUT THE AUTHOR

Heather Flood was encouraged to write by her husband Tony, a former journalist.

She began by reviewing theatrical productions for the Richmond and Twickenham Times series and still pens theatre reviews for the Brighton Argus.

Heather gave Tony the idea for his first children's novel, The Secret Potion, and then decided to write children's books herself, mainly for her grandchildren

Gabrielle- Antonia and Ashlee, and, more recently, little Samuel. Heather has benefited from belonging to the Anderida Writers Group in Eastbourne, with whom she has won awards, and meeting publishers Rupert Barlow and Rex Sumner, who has offered help and advice through his company My Voice Publishing.

She also loves singing and belongs to the Concentus singers. Heather enjoys new challenges. These include helping her first husband build three houses, climbing The Great Wall of China and making celebration cakes. She and Tony also run the Alice Croft House Creative Writing Group.

You can find news about Heather and Tony's books on **www.fantasyadventurebooks.com**.

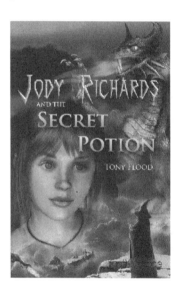

THE SECRET POTION

Readers pining for more magic post Harry Potter need look no further. Tony Flood has conjured up all the wizards, witches, goblins, pixies and poisonous spiders you could want, and quite possibly the world's worst monster.

So says best-selling author Jessica Duchen and actress June Whitfield when recommending Tony's fantastic book about Jody Richards' mind-boggling adventures.

When her brother is kidnapped by a wicked wizard,10-year-old Jody sets out to look for him. Her quest carries her to a dreamland named Tamila, chock-full of wizards, witches and whirlpools, where drama and danger abound. But there is plenty of humour, too, and good eventually triumphs over evil.

The Secret Potion is available on Amazon Books UK as either a paperback or e-version, or signed copies by author Tony Flood can be obtained from: **www.fantasyadventurebooks.com**

Look out for special offers of signed books on

www.fantasyadventurebooks.com

Printed in Great Britain
by Amazon